SCOOBY DOO™

MOVIE SCRAPBOOK

By Monica Rizzo

SCHOLASTIC INC.

New York   Toronto   London   Auckland   Sydney   Mexico City

New Delhi   Hong Kong   Buenos Aires

No part of this publication may be reproduced in whole or in part, or stored in a retrieval system, or transmitted in any form or by any means, electronic, mechanical, photocopying, recording, or otherwise, without written permission of the publisher. For information regarding permission, write to Scholastic Inc., Attention: Permissions Department, 557 Broadway, New York, NY 10012.

ISBN 0-439-35496-X

Cover Design: Louise Bova

Interior Design: Kay Petronio

12 11 10 9 8 7 6 5 4 3   2 3 4 5 6 7/0

Printed in the U.S.A.

First Scholastic printing, May 2002

Hello and welcome, mystery lovers! This is it — your backstage pass to the making of the Scooby-Doo movie. You'll get behind-the-scenes access to the stars, the story, the set, the director and producer, and the special effects people who brought that lovable cartoon dog to life for the very first time. And at the end of the book, you can match your Scooby smarts against the stars of the movie. So hop into the Mystery Machine — the adventure is about to begin!

INSIDER INFO

Scooby-Doo is one of the most popular cartoons in television history. Created by the legendary animation team of William Hanna and Joseph Barbera, America's most beloved Great Dane and his four mystery-loving pals debuted in 1969 with the series *Scooby-Doo, Where Are You?* The show was an instant hit, and since then, it's become a classic. For years, the cartoon series dominated Saturday mornings in homes all around the U.S. These days, you can watch the show over 70 times a week on Cartoon Network.

Director Raja Gosnell with the cast of the Scooby movie.

THE FIRST MOVIE

So the question is, why hasn't Scooby made it to the big screen before now? According to producer Charles Roven, it's because it's never been possible to make Scooby really *real* — until now. "The reason to do a Scooby-Doo movie is really to take advantage of the fantastic computer effects that have been developed over the last several years," Charles says. "We wanted to be able to make a lifelike Scooby and show what he would be in a live-action film [that is, with actors instead of cartoons]. That is a really exciting challenge — to be able to give people a real three-dimensional look at what this dog and this gang would be if they were around in the real world."

First and foremost, Charles and director Raja Gosnell wanted to stay true to the cartoon. "There is a lot of responsibility when you take something that people are familiar with," Charles says.

That meant casting four actors who were as into Scooby as the filmmakers were. Of the cast members, Freddie Prinze, Jr. was probably the biggest fan of the cartoon series. At first

he didn't seem like a natural for the role of Mystery, Inc. leader Fred Jones. After all, Fred Jones is a golden-haired blond, and Freddie has dark brown hair. But once he met with the producer and director, it was clear he was perfect for the part. "He has seen every single Scooby-Doo cartoon ever made," Charles says. "For him the [character] research maybe was his whole life."

Filling the designer shoes of "damsel in distress" Daphne Blake is Sarah Michelle Gellar, best known for her lead role as the kick-butt heroine on *Buffy the Vampire Slayer*. Sarah was the perfect blend of beautiful *and* bold — because in the film, unlike the cartoon, danger-prone Daphne shows the gang she can hold her own against the bad guys.

Finding the perfect Shaggy was a challenge, until Matthew Lillard walked into the audition room. Physically, he resembled the lanky, Scooby snack-loving dude from the cartoon. But more importantly, says producer Richard Suckle, "he didn't try to come in and imitate Shaggy's voice. He brought some of the Shaggyisms as well as Matthew Lillard. It was a fantastic mix that made it feel

Linda and Freddie are on the case.

Rowan Atkinson plays Emile Mondavarious, the amusement park owner who brings the gang together again.

natural when he was playing the character."

The same was true for Linda Cardellini, who plays the role of Velma Dinkley, the brains behind Mystery, Inc. "It's almost scary when she walks on set," Richard says. "You look at Linda and it's like there's Velma Dinkley standing right in your face."

Actor Rowan Atkinson, whom moviegoers know as the quirky and humorous Mr. Bean, rounds out the main cast as Emile Mondavarious, the owner of the amusement park Spooky Island.

A poster for Spooky Island, the location of the Scooby gang's latest case.

A NEW STORY

When we first catch up with the Mystery, Inc. gang, we learn that after years of solving mysteries together, they've gotten sick and tired of one another. So they all go their separate ways. Fred becomes a one-man publicity machine, writing books about himself and his days with Mystery Inc. Daphne, tired of being kidnapped by guys in masks, decides to learn martial arts. Super-sleuth Velma gets a job as

a rocket scientist at NASA. At least Shaggy and Scooby are still together — they're living in California in the back of the Mystery Machine, barbecuing and selling pottery.

But the gang finds themselves together again when they all receive the same letter asking them to help solve a mystery on a place called Spooky Island. After some consideration — and some quarreling — they agree to band together for the mission. They head off to Spooky Island. And that's where the fun really begins — only this time, instead of unmasking men in costume, the gang finds themselves hot on the trail of *real* ghosts and demons.

Director Raja Gosnell promises that viewers won't be disappointed. "I think we have elements in there for everyone because they are going to love Scooby, love Shaggy, love the action, love the physical comedy. I wanted to make the movie big and hip and fun . . . what the whole family can enjoy."

Sarah Michelle Gellar as Daphne Blake

CHAPTER ONE

MEET SARAH MICHELLE GELLAR "DAPHNE BLAKE"

Daphne seems like she's got it all together. Her strawberry blonde hair is styled perfectly, her clothes are hip and sharp, and she's always friendly and cheerful. But sometimes she doesn't make the wisest of choices, which lead others to question her street smarts. She often has bright ideas for solving mysteries, but she just seems to attract danger wherever she goes. Her unenviable position of "damsel in distress" often gives the Mystery, Inc. another mission in addition to solving the mystery — rescuing Daphne.

"Daphne is often perceived as a stereotypical pretty girl," Sarah Michelle Gellar explains. "She's the kind of person that didn't always believe in herself because people tended to judge her exterior without looking any further."

This time around, though, Daphne decides to change all of that and, says Sarah, learns "how to make herself an important and intricate part of the group."

Playing a strong, empowered young woman is something Sarah has a lot of experience with. On her hit television show *Buffy the Vampire Slayer*, Sarah fights evil on a weekly basis. Her fight scenes on *Buffy* were great preparation for the movie, in which Daphne fights off would-be kidnappers like an old pro.

Sarah promises fans won't be disappointed with the "new" Daphne because she still has

Mark McGrath of Sugar Ray serenades Daphne (Sarah).

the same traits and characteristics as in the cartoon. Only now, Sarah says, she's "more her own person."

SARAH ON SCOOBY: A Q&A

Were you nervous about playing such a well-known and loved cartoon character?

It's a real challenge to play someone as iconic as Daphne. So many people worldwide have an ideal of who Daphne is and how she's supposed to be. You're walking a fine line because everyone knows Daphne as a two-dimensional cartoon character and now you're taking her into a three-dimensional feature film.

ished reading the script I said, "This is fabulous! They did everything that needed to be done." The innuendo and humor kept the integrity of the cartoon, and it was incredibly funny, witty and real.

How true to the cartoon is the movie?

I think it's been very important to all of us to keep the characters true. This is especially so in terms of physical appearance, although my Daphne does change clothes where the cartoon Daphne never does. The mentality of the character is also very faithful. Daphne is always the one in trouble, needing rescue. And Fred and the gang are always there to save her.

That said, how do you take such a well-loved cartoon and make it into a movie?

I read the script with a lot of curiosity. How do you handle all the different stories? Where does it begin and end? How do you bring the characters into modern day? Or do you? How do you make them into three-dimensional characters? When I fin-

What is it about Scooby-Doo that has helped it endure for more than 30 years?

I think everybody is a Scooby-Doo fan. In the past, superheroes were superheroes, and this

was one of the first cartoons that was really made for everybody — girl, boy, young, old. I think that's exactly what's kept it popular for all these years. You can't aim something at just one group and make it transcend all those generations and all those different groups. It has to be something for everyone, something everyone sees, whether it's in each character or in the story.

What's it like working on such a big production for six months?

It's an amazing flow. It starts from Raja, who is the most incredible director I have ever worked with. I have never worked with someone that just wants everything to be great and everyone to have a good time. The cast works incredibly well together. It's supportive. It's creative. It's a really great environment to work in. It's really easy to turn to someone else and go, "This isn't working" or "What do you think?" or "How do you think this would work?" And more so than any other project, it's been an incredible group effort.

How was this group of actors to work with?

Matthew is a walking incarnation of Shaggy. I've known him for a long time and it's been such a great chance to observe him and his acting process. He brings a new idea to each take,

which is wonderful to play with. And I've always had the utmost respect for Freddie as an actor. Working with him has been great and easy. Linda makes a great Velma. She has this incredible sarcastic humor that's perfect for the role. And she's an incredible Scooby fan and brings so much heart into the project and into the character, because this is a character that she truly loves.

Do you think audiences will like the film?

To see Scooby on the big screen will be incredible. He's your dog. It's unbelievable. The film has the perfect feel--the ambience, the color schemes, the costumes, the set. It all falls into place just right. That's the excitement of seeing this movie.

The movie begins with Daphne being kidnapped — her classic "damsel in distress" moment.

Date of Birth: April 14, 1977

Hometown: Born and raised in New York City

Breakthrough role: Played a young Jacqueline Bouvier (Kennedy) in the television movie *A Woman Named Jackie*

Trophy Girl: In 1995, Sarah received a Daytime Emmy Award for her role as Erica Kane's (Susan Lucci) daughter on the soap opera *All My Children*. In 2001, she was nominated for a Golden Globe Award in the Best Actress category for *Buffy the Vampire Slayer*.

Favorite Scooby Snack: Sushi

Screen Gems: In addition to Sarah's two high-profile television roles on *All My Children* and *Buffy*, she's also graced the big screen in feature films like *I Know What You Did Last Summer*, *Cruel Intentions*, and *Scream 2*.

Freddie Prinze, Jr. as Fred Jones, the unofficial leader of the gang

As the leader of the Mystery Inc. crew, Fred Jones has an image to uphold. He's strong, confident, and authoritative at times. He's like the most popular guy in school — good-looking, athletic, and even smart. Obviously, he was the perfect role for actor/heartthrob Freddie Prinze, Jr., who has the same easy confidence and likeability. Not to mention that Freddie's been a huge fan of Scooby-Doo since he was a little kid. He has a large collection of Scooby memorabilia, including the entire cartoon catalog on videotape.

But interestingly, Freddie didn't jump at the chance to play his cartoon idol. In fact, he couldn't bear the thought of seeing his favorite cartoon brought to the big screen. "I was hesitant because I'm such a huge fan of the Scooby-Doo series. I didn't want to be part of the film project unless it matched the quality of the cartoon."

At first, Freddie wouldn't even look at the script for fear it would tarnish his love for the cartoon. But after his girlfriend (now fiancée), Sarah Michelle Gellar, accepted the role of Daphne Blake, Freddie changed his mind. Sarah convinced him that the movie would bring the cartoon to life in an exciting and visually stunning way. After a quick call to his agent and a meeting with director Raja Gosnell, Freddie was able to reclaim the role before it got away from him.

It was a close call, he says now. "I would have missed out on a great opportunity," Freddie says. "I'm thrilled to be part of this film. This is the kind of movie that lasts forever. Kids will watch it for the next fifty years."

FREDDIE ON FRED — AND MORE!

Rumor has it you're a big Scooby-Doo fan.
Over the years, I have collected every episode of Scooby-Doo that has ever come

out on tape. I am a true fan. I was very fond of it as a child and am still now. It's this gang of friends who are all very different people but use their differences to fight crime and solve mysteries. Plus, they had a cool talking dog — and how can you go wrong with that?

Fred is the leader of the group. But at times he can be a little smug, don't you think?

Fred is a good guy. He's just a little behind the times. What makes him so lovable and goofy is that he thinks he's got it all down.

You had to dye your dark brown hair blond for the movie. Was that fun?

That was the one difficult thing about making this movie. I didn't like the blond hair. I would go as far as saying I hated it. The process of bleaching blackish-brown hair is very, very time-consuming and damaging. My hair grows like a weed so we had to go through the root-bleaching process every nine days. My hair was so fried. It became like hay that I could feed to some animals on a

nearby ranch. After we were done filming, I knew I had to shave it all off and start over. On the last day of filming, I went over to the director with a razor in my hand and I said, "You're sure we're done, right?" The hair came off that day.

What if there's a sequel?

I would do a sequel if it was the same group of cast and crew, but I would probably argue that Fred would like to have brown hair for that one.

You, Matthew, and Sarah already knew each other before filming began. And you all met Linda for the first time. How did everyone get along for the six months that you were on location in Australia?

It was a great chance to work with Matt again. I have always been of the opinion that Matt makes my work better. I hope I do the same for him in return. And I feel the same way about Sarah. It was like a bunch of friends getting together to make a movie and hang out in a foreign country. We got paid to portray friends while hanging out with our real friends.

Freddie and Matt on set together — this is the friends' fourth movie together.

The friendship part of the Scooby gang came naturally. There was no getting to know you period. Linda fit into the picture perfectly. I'm not sure what she expected when she got there, but she quickly realized how laid back we were and became part of the gang instantly.

You've got a reputation as a practical joker. Did you pull any on the Scooby gang?

Once I turned on the heater for four hours on a hot day and Matt came back to a roasting trailer. (Laughing.) That's why I love working with him. I have played pranks on him from day one of knowing each other and he never knows it's me. It's gotten too easy. It's like beating up your little brother. I finally 'fessed up on this film and he was surprised. The challenge was gone.

What did you do in your free time?

I'm writing a comic book of my own and I spent a lot of my free time on set coming up with ideas, creating my characters and the world they are going to live in. On weekends, we'd all get together and eat big meals and rent movies. Or Sarah and I would fly to Sydney and hang out in the big city. We caught a Kylie Minogue concert. It was crazy. They love her in Australia. It's like seeing Prince in America.

What's your favorite scene from the movie?

Without a doubt, it was the scene called the soul-switching scene. All of the characters have their souls switched by an evil force.

When the movie begins, Fred is promoting his new book, *Fred on Fred: The Many Faces of Me.*

Freddie — as Daphne!

We got to all play a different character or two for a few minutes in the film. I get to be Velma, and it was fun to see Matt do me. He used it as his opportunity to try and poke fun at the things I say and the gestures I make. We each had to figure out the quirks that would clue the audience into who we were at that point when the souls are switched. It was fun, but I definitely make a better Fred than Velma.

Since you're such a big Scooby fan, did you keep any props from the movie?

I kept a fire hose that Fred uses in a fight and does some kung-fu moves with.

You didn't keep Fred's trademark ascot tie?

I most certainly didn't keep the ascot. That thing was uncomfortable and itchy. The costumer and I decided we should hold a ritual burning of the ascot at the end of filming. As modern as we made the movie, there are certain things that just had to be kept. So as much as I hated the scarf, it had to stay. It is a piece of Fred. We crack jokes about the ascot in the movie.

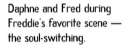

Daphne and Fred during Freddie's favorite scene — the soul-switching.

Date of Birth: March 8, 1976

Hometown: Born in Los Angeles, raised in Albuquerque, New Mexico

Breakthrough role: Played Claire Danes' boyfriend in *To Gillian on Her 37th Birthday* (1996)

Hobbies: Freddie loves to cook, play basketball, and collect comic books.

Favorite Scooby Snack: Pizza and Italian food. "I am always hungry," Freddie says.

Screen Gems: Freddie has starred in many of Hollywood's top teen movies including *I Know What You Did Last Summer, I Still Know What You Did Last Summer, She's All That, Wing Commander, Head Over Heels,* and *Summer Catch.*

Matthew Lillard brings the cartoon character Shaggy to life for the first time

Shaggy is the kind of easy-going, food-loving soul that no one can help liking. He goes with the flow, traveling the country in the Mystery Machine with Scooby-Doo, his best friend in food and fear. He's such a fun, down-to-earth guy, it's no wonder Matthew Lillard was jumping for joy at the chance to portray him on the big screen.

"Shaggy is such a big icon, such a great character, that it's hard to say no to those opportunities," says Matthew, who, like his co-star Freddie Prinze, Jr., has been a fan of the cartoon since childhood. "I'd come home from fifth, sixth, seventh grade and turn it on. It was always on. It was great. If anyone had ever told me I was going to play Shaggy in a big movie, I would have told them they were crazy."

While Matthew considered himself lucky to get the chance to star in such a big movie, he knew it would be hard work. "I was really nervous because you don't want to be the guy who screws up Shaggy," Matthew says. "I wanted to do the best job I could. There was a lot of pressure on me. I had an idea of what I wanted to do, because I'd watched the cartoon for so long. When I got the part I pretty much watched every single one of them ever made, so I knew what he was like, and I wanted to bring that to life."

Fans won't be disappointed. Just as he wowed moviegoers with his hilarious performances in *Scream* and *She's All That*, fans of the Scooby-Doo cartoon will love Matthew's portrayal of Shaggy. "If you love the cartoon and you grew up a fan of that, then this is a must-see. It's all the things you loved about the cartoon in a full-length movie. It's got a great story, great characters, a couple of twists in the end that are fun. It's great fun for a whole family."

Matthew perfectly captures one of Shaggy's trademark emotions — fear!

Matthew and director Raja Gosnell — the two got along great on set.

things because I'd never done anything like this before. I'd never done an accent or an impression in a movie. So to do one of this size and this stature and with this high profile of a part to start with was intimidating, to say the least.

How hard was it to talk in Shaggy's trademark voice?

When I first started working on the voice of Shaggy I would have to scream for a long time to get my voice tired, so that I could talk with a scratchy voice. You can't really go through six months of work screaming yourself hoarse to sound like Shaggy. I did that originally to get the part, and then when I did, I figured that I would have to find a better way to do the voice. I started to work with my own voice to find the break [scratchy quality] in Shaggy's voice.

Shaggy (Matthew) arrives at Spooky Island.

MATTHEW ON SCOOBY SNACKS, SHAGGY-SPEAK, AND MORE!

Did you have a Shaggy imitation before you got the part?

Oh no, in fact, I never did any imitations before I got the role. That was one of the scariest

Matthew in one of the movie's weirder scenes — trapped by sausages!

What kind of input did you have with helping work out your character?

The great thing about Raja [Gosnell, the director] is we talked about what we wanted to do with the part and we agreed early on. I would do a scene and I'd do it again the way that he wanted it, kind of the safer version. Then he let me go off and attack it and improvise. It was a two to one — he'd get two [takes] and I'd get one. And that was great because that will allow you as an actor to be creative and create a fuller character. It's a really great way of working.

Shaggy and Scooby are best friends and share a love for crime-solving and eating. Are you as food-obsessed as Shaggy?

No, I'm not as food obsessed, but I sure do like chocolate chip cookies. At one point somebody said, "Let's give Shaggy a cheeseburger." And I said "No, no, no. Shaggy's a veggie head." But I'm not. I like a good cheeseburger.

Did you have to eat a lot of Scooby Snacks in the movie?

That's funny, because they asked us at one point, "What do you want your Scooby Snacks to be made out of?" And I was like, "Just make it healthy." So they made them out of this oats and grains kind of stuff. They were terrible. Any time you see me eating a Scooby Snack in the movie, they were miserable. But they looked good on camera.

What was one of your favorite scenes?

Well, there was a big fart contest between Scooby-Doo and me. I liked that. Also, Shaggy gets a girlfriend in the movie. Her name is Mary Jane, and she's played by Isla Fisher. That was fun. To play Shaggy getting the girl was a blast.

Matthew, as Shaggy, is often scared, but he always has the courage to face his fears.

There were a lot of stunts in the movie. Were they hard to do?

It was really hard because given the circumstances of the characters, they're running for their lives in the entire film, just like in the cartoon. I mean, the gang is being chased by bad guys almost the entire time. You add the fact that you're playing a cartoon character and the amount of energy that goes into representing that cartoon character truthfully is pretty extreme. It was an exhausting and long shoot. But it's a big movie so because of that, the bigger the movie the longer it takes.

All the pretty hard core stunts a stunt guy did. But the small stuff I did. In one scene there's a tube I go down to save Scooby, so they kind of hooked me onto these wires as they sent me down this tube. It was kind of like a waterslide only it was covered in slime. I went down it about twenty to thirty feet. It was at such an angle that I went down really fast and they had built this platform [mats at the end of the slide] and I went diving into the platform of mats. It was totally fun. Any time you get to do physical stuff like that it's totally fun. The acting is great, but when you get to do the physical stuff on top of it, it makes it that much more exciting.

This was a particularly long movie shoot. What did you all do during your free time?

We did everything. The set was right next door to an amusement park. We shot at a place in the Gold Coast called Movieland, kind of like a Universal Studios with roller coasters. So every now and then we would pop over and ride the roller coasters. One night off we played tag with Nerf guns at Freddie's house.

Sounds like making this movie was more fun than it was work.

When you're working with people you know and like, that makes your job so much better. There is so much down time that you can enjoy each other's company in between shots and on the weekends. They're such great people, so down to earth.

Date of Birth: January 24, 1970

Hometown: Born in Lansing, Michigan. Moved to Tustin, California, as a young boy.

Early Gig: Hosted the Nickelodeon series *SK8 TV* in 1989

Breakthrough Role: Played a high school student in *Scream* (1996)

Hobbies: He's a big fan of the theater, where he first trained to become an actor.

Favorite Scooby Snack: Nacho cheese Doritos. "The cheesier the better," Matthew says.

Screen Gems: Matthew has appeared in numerous films, including *Scream, Hackers, She's All That, Wing Commander, SLC Punk, Summer Catch,* and *13 Ghosts.*

Linda Cardellini as brainiac Velma Dinkley

What would Mystery, Inc. be without Velma Dinkley? The smartest member of the group, she always offers the group innovative, intelligent insight, but she rarely gets the credit when her ideas pan out. However, that doesn't prevent the preppy brainiac from going about her work, which often involves bribing Shaggy and Scooby with Scooby Snacks.

As a child, actress Linda Cardellini confesses that she was more drawn to Daphne than Velma. It wasn't until she got older that she changed her mind. "As a little girl, I thought Daphne was so pretty and she dressed the best. I wanted to be her. No one wanted to be Velma," Linda explains. "But in reality, Velma manages to be the uncool cool girl. In simple terms, she's just smart. She loves what she does, and she's comfortable with who she is. She doesn't worry about what she wears and she just is how she is. I find her the most interesting."

This isn't the first time Linda has played the smart girl. In 1999, she starred as straight-A student Lindsay Weir on the critically acclaimed TV show *Freaks and Geeks*. Since then, Linda has gone back to college in Los Angeles, where she's majoring in theater.

Fortunately, Linda was able to take the necessary time off to work on the Scooby

Linda's Velma has a bit more dimension than the classic character.

movie. She says she wouldn't have missed it for the world. "I love Scooby-Doo! How could I not be Velma?" she asks. "I'm so fortunate to have the opportunity. Bringing her to real life is hard and it's a lot of pressure. But it's fun."

LINDA ON VELMA — THE INSIDE SCOOP

Were you a fan of the cartoon?
Scooby-Doo was my favorite cartoon when I was a kid, and it still is. I liked any episode

that had Don Knotts in it. Those were classic.

What do you like about the movie that's different from the cartoon series?

We start in the midst of a mystery, which is classic Scooby. We have a little separation of the gang, and you get to see into the personal lives of the characters, which you never saw in the old cartoons. You find out I work at NASA on the side. You get to see what else the five of us at Mystery, Inc. do in our spare time.

What kinds of things did you do to make yourself look so much like Velma from the cartoon?

I have the Coke bottle glasses, I had to wear the familiar orange turtleneck, although they went with a little different skirt and shoes. The ones they chose were a little updated. I also had to cut my hair. I have had long hair my whole life and for six months I had the

Velma helmet hairdo. Everyone thinks it was a wig, so I probably should have just worn one and saved my hair from the chopping block. It took an hour with an expert hairstylist and a lot of hairspray to get that helmet perfect every day.

I re-watched all the cartoons. I borrowed a lot of them on tape from Raja [Gosnell, the director]. I called and talked to the woman who was the original voice of Velma. She really didn't think there was much she could tell me, but just talking to her was really fascinating. It was monumental to talk to the woman who originated Velma's voice. There were a ton of Velma and Shaggy lines on the Internet, so my boyfriend burned them onto a CD and left a long pause after each one, so it was like a language tape. I could repeat after her, which really helped me get down the certain cadence Velma has in her voice.

As the group's resident brains, Velma and Fred can't help being a little jealous of each other.

You said you liked Daphne better when you were a kid. if you had a choice, would you have preferred to portray her in the movie?

A couple of years ago, my friends and I were going to dress up as the Scooby gang for Halloween, and no one wanted to be Velma. The two girls in the group were fighting over Daphne until I gave in and said I'd be Velma. Then I realized how much fun it would be to be Velma. She is a very complex character, and the smartest one of the bunch. There was so much you could do with her. We never ended up doing it, but I guess it got me hungry to play Velma. It was fate, I guess.

What's your favorite scene from the movie?

My favorite scene is the one at the Voodoo Lounge. I get to sing and dance. The scene is meant to be an out-of-character moment for Velma. I got to be funny in this part. That scene is the best because she breaks from her norm and out of her shell. I worked with a singing coach and a choreographer. It was a fun departure from what I was doing for most of the five and a half months I was in Australia.

The Scooby cartoons were known for celebrity cameos, and this movie is no different. Tell us about working with Pam Anderson, and the hit band Sugar Ray.

Having real-life celebrity guest stars on a cartoon was a fantastic idea and particularly innovative at the time. And they always got the people on there who were big at the time. They were the people you'd want to see on *The Tonight Show*. They decided to have a few real-life celebs do a few cameos, and they got some great people. When

Linda having a classic Velma moment — looking for her glasses.

It is always hard to be the new kid. Everybody was really sweet to me. They are very welcoming into their circle.

How did you spend your down time in Australia?

I loved my life there. It was beautiful. I was so close to the beach at all times, and the beaches there are so vast and gorgeous. The sunsets are beautiful. We went to the beach a lot and I hung out with my friend Judy. My family came to visit and I showed them around. The cast would play games together and eat together.

The island that stands in for Spooky Island was a paradise. We got to feed wild dolphins, which was a first for me. You don't get to pet them though. They have to keep them wild so they will feed themselves and live on their own. It was really lush and the water was so beautiful.

Sugar Ray came, we had been on the island for so long that it was just nice to see new faces. Pamela came during one of the very first weeks of shooting. She was fun to work with.

Did you keep any souvenirs from the movie?

I took home my glasses, my orange turtleneck, skirt, and shoes. Pretty much I could be Velma for Halloween next year. I put it on and give myself advice in front of the mirror on bad days. I also kept one of the dolls from the Wow-O toy factory scene and it is autographed "To Velma Love Pam Anderson." That is cool. As a wrap gift, we were all given a statue of the Luna Ghost from the film. It looks all billowy and sinewy. I also came home with a bicycle I used to ride around Australia.

How was it working with Freddie, Sarah, and Matthew? They were already friends before the movie, but you didn't meet them until shooting started.

Linda with some of the movie's spookier characters.

Date of Birth: June 25

Hometown: Linda was born and raised in Northern California. She moved to Los Angeles after high school to pursue acting full time.

Early Passion: Linda has been involved in community and school theater since the age of ten.

Stroke of Luck: Linda was once a contestant on *The Price Is Right* game show, and won a brand-new fireplace.

Breakthrough Role: She starred as smart but cool high schooler Lindsay Weir on the critically acclaimed television series *Freaks and Geeks* in 1998.

Favorite Scooby Snack: "I love donuts. I'm a sucker for white cake, white frosting, and rainbow sprinkles, although I wouldn't turn away a perfectly good glazed," Linda says.

Screen Gems: Linda appeared in the films *Good Burger* and *Dead Man on Campus*, and guest-starred in a number of television shows including *The Lot*, *Boy Meets World*, *Clueless*, *Step by Step*, and *3rd Rock From the Sun*, before landing a lead role on *Freaks and Geeks*.

The all-new Scooby looks like a real dog, but acts human in many ways — just like the cartoon Scooby

MEET THE MAKERS
OF THE NEW SCOOBY-DOO

Getting the world's most beloved Great Dane camera-ready for his first live-action feature film was a huge challenge for the makers of the Scooby movie. At first, they wondered if a real animal could take on the role. But the animated Scooby is so human in so many ways — his paws are like hands, he walks on his two hind legs, and he even talks like a real person — the film's producers and director knew they would have to find another way to bring Scooby to life.

"It was very important for me that Scooby looked and acted like a real dog, because he has to inhabit this real world," explains director Raja Gosnell. "I didn't want to do an animated character. It looked great in *Who Framed Roger Rabbit* — one of my favorite movies — but they created this whole world where 'toons existed. We don't have that sort of cartoon world [for Scooby-Doo]."

So to make Scooby seem really *real*, visual effects supervisor Peter Crossman and his staff got to work on creating a computer generated image (CGI) of Scooby-Doo for the big screen. The crew watched dozens of old Scooby episodes to get a grasp on how he fits into his world — how he walks, talks, laughs, and *especially* how he runs. They drew sketches of how Scooby would fit into scenes with the actors playing the rest of the gang. Then those images were made into animated, cartoon

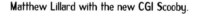

Matthew Lillard with the new CGI Scooby.

form. With help from the Warner Bros. Feature Animation department, as well as outside special effects company Rhythm & Hues (who created Babe the pig in the movie *Babe*), a computer-generated Scooby was born.

Next, the crew had to "block" scenes with the actors. That is, they had to see just how much room a 70-lb dog would need onscreen when responding to the different situations in the film.

One difficult task Rhythm & Hues faced was making sure the CGI Scooby fit seamlessly into the film. His eyes had to make contact with the others actors in the scene, he had to be lit and shadowed the same way the other actors were, and most of all, he had to look *alive*. Rhythm & Hues first scanned a scaled, animated wire frame image onto the computer, then added the animal's muscles and fur. A staff of nearly fifteen animators and computer graphics specialists worked on this aspect of the film for nearly a year.

One of the most difficult scenes to illustrate was a fight between Shaggy and Scooby. The director wanted to shoot the scene with a Steadicam, which moves with the actors in the scene. This was a really tough job for actor Matthew Lillard, who had to pretend he was fighting with someone who wasn't there, but it was also very challenging for the graphics specialists.

"Scooby's performance had to be very fluid on the ground," Crossman explains. "Whenever we are pinning a computer-generated character to the ground, we have to do a lot of copying of reality into the three-dimensional space to make sure that Scooby's feet meet the ground — that he can throw shadows on the ground, just the way real performers do in the real world."

Other challenges for the filmmakers were showing Scooby wearing a dress, Scooby climbing a palm tree, Scooby driving a motorbike, and Scooby frightened by demons. After all, he wouldn't be Scooby if he weren't scared out of his wits half the time. "I'm always drawn to the comedic side of visual effects," Crossman says. "I think when you get the combination of the supernatural and the comedic in movies like *Ghostbusters* and that sort of thing, it's the penultimate kind of effects movie to work on. These are all things that read wonderfully for a TV animated cartoon, but the idea of making them happen cinematically is pretty challenging. We love those challenges."

Date of Birth: Unknown, though he first appeared with the Mystery, Inc. gang on September 13, 1969

Hometown: The road, which he travels with Shaggy in the Mystery Machine.

Passion: Eating as much as possible, as often as possible.

Favorite Foods: Scooby Snacks, pizza, ice cream, and whatever Shaggy can't finish.

Distinguishable characteristics: Opposable thumbs that work like human thumbs, the ability to speak.

Favorite Phrases: "Ruh-roh" and "Scooby Snack"

CHAPTER SIX

HOW'D THEY DO THAT?
THE SPECIAL EFFECTS

Creating a believable Scooby-Doo (described in chapter five) for the big screen was just the beginning for the special effects staff working on the Scooby-Doo movie. They wanted to make the movie as visually exciting and action-packed as the cartoon, and to do that, they knew they would have to come up with the wildest-possible special effects.

THE GHOSTS, DEMONS, AND GHOULIES

Bill Kent, the animation supervisor for Warner Bros., and his staff worked tirelessly to create the many demons and ghosts that haunt the Mystery, Inc. gang in the movie. The first part of putting together believable demons is creat-ing their look, which has to be similar to the look of the movie's setting. The darker and more mysterious the setting, the darker and more menacing the demon.

Next, says Kent, is giving the demons their personalities. "What we bring to the table is humor and character animation," Kent explains. "We're hoping to get real performances — the puzzled look, the physical look, the ferocious look. We try and make them frightening but not over-whelming."

The studio created plaster masks of the demons to give Kent and his crew a base from which to operate when incorporating them into computer graphics. That went a long way toward making them look as real as possible — and as terrifying as possible!

A cool mask from the movie.

Some of the creepy-looking sets built for the movie.

SPOOKY HOTEL

says. "In some scenes, we have so many layers to put together. Our biggest challenge is to make them not look just inserted into the scene, but make them *part* of the scene."

"The most challenging aspect of being an actor is to perform with a character who isn't physically there," Freddie Prinze, Jr. (Fred Jones) says. "Your eyes have to focus on something that isn't there. I always say that if you played cowboys and Indians you can be an actor."

Actor Miguel A. Nuñez, who played the Voodoo Maestro, with a spooky-looking totem from the movie.

The Spooky Island hotel has a unique look.

THE ACTION

Action scenes involving the demons had many steps. For example, in one scene, the demons fly into Dead Mike's bar, breaking a wall and a window, and the Scooby gang all runs away. So first, the film-makers had to shoot the wall and window intact — that is, unbroken. Then windscreen machines were set up behind the wall to help shatter the plaster and the fake window glass, and blow it in one direction, to give the illusion that something was flying through it from one side. After that, the director had to film the actors being chased away and *then* film just the demon crashing through the wall. Once all the filming was done, all the different layers were pieced together to make it look like one fluid scene. And that's just *one* scene in a movie filled with cool special effects!

"It becomes complex at times," Kent

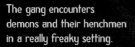

The gang encounters demons and their henchmen in a really freaky setting.

One scene set on Spooky Island, the creepy amusement park where most of the movie takes place, required the kids from Mystery, Inc. to stretch their imaginations to the utmost. When they encounter an evil force that switches all of their souls, Fred becomes Velma, Shaggy becomes Fred, Velma becomes Daphne, and so on. A digital effect of the gang's souls swirling around the actors, jumping in and out of their bodies, would be added later. The scene required the actors to improvise quite a bit — they had to act like their souls were flying out of them and switching around while nothing was really there. Then the special effects team had to digitally

generate the souls circling the actors, choreographing their every move with that of the actors to make it look like it was a completely natural thing to happen.

While all of these complicated effects took almost a year to complete, Kent says it is ultimately rewarding and fun. "We've got some funny gags in the movie. We've got a shot where Velma [Linda Cardellini] is actually picked up by a demon, and she tries to stand on his mouth and pull on his ears," Kent says, laughing. The shot was filmed with a large blue screen behind Velma, while she hung on a wire to make it look like she was interacting with the demon. Later on, computer

Sarah gets captured by a demon suspended from wires. The wires will be removed digitally.

graphics of the demon were added to complement Velma's range of expressions and actions.

THE STUNTS

Many of the special effects scenes were enhanced by hooking the actors onto cable wires. In one scene, Daphne (Sarah Michelle Gellar) has to fight the evil Zarkos (played by actor Sam Greco). As their face-off intensifies, Daphne engages in a series of complex martial arts maneuvers, enhanced by a wire technique made popular in the films *Crouching Tiger, Hidden Dragon* and *Charlie's Angels*.

Stunt Supervisor Guy Norris says the scene ultimately worked well because of Sarah's skills and determination. "Traditionally, you have to have a situation where you have your leading actress or actor walk in and do a couple of close ups, and the rest of it is left to the stunt crew," Norris says. Stunts can be so difficult — and dangerous — for actors who are not trained in how to perform physically without getting hurt. But in this case, it was a bit different. "Fortunately, because of the amount of training we had to do with Sarah, and her own physical ability, we could put on wires, have her swing through the air doing somer-

Hanging from a wire, Sarah fights Zarkos. The wire will be removed from the film in post-production.

saults, and do all the things you can't usually get actors to do," says Norris. "That gives the scene that little bit extra in the final sequence when you're editing it."

Sarah, for one, is happy she stuck with it. "It's hard work and it's fun," she says. "All the wire work was really new to me, but the wire team is unbelievable. The moves they can do, the agility with which they do it, the strength they have has such beauty.

Every move has meaning."

But not every move was without its drawbacks, says Sarah. "It's been an incredibly physical role," Sarah says. "Daphne has been a challenge for me, and for the makeup department to cover my bruises!"

In the end, Matthew says it was all worth it. "We had a blast making the movie, so hopefully people will have as much fun seeing it as we had making it."

CHAPTER SEVEN

BEHIND THE SCENES

The cast chats with Rowan Atkinson on a beautiful sunny day in Australia.

Working on a full-length feature film involves a lot of hard work from the cast and crew. The Scooby-Doo movie took six months to film, and another ten months of post-production. That's when the computer images of Scooby-Doo and the demons were added, and when a lot of scenes are "cleaned up" — which involves removing all the guide wires used for stunts in several scenes (like Daphne's big martial arts duel).

The entire movie was filmed on location in Brisbane, Australia, which is located in the eastern region of the country. It's also called the Gold Coast because it has some of the area's most lush and geographically diverse landscapes, from beautiful sandy beaches to hilly, dense forests. It was the perfect background for Mystery, Inc.'s adventures. Director Raja Gosnell says the land down under was a great film location because "it has incredible geological differences and advantages. There's the rain forest, the beaches, and of course some amazing outback locations. It's a really nice place to come and make a movie. The people are great, the crews are great. There's the rain forest, the beaches — all within driving distance."

But not everything the film needed could be found in Brisbane. They needed a Spooky Island. The perfect location was Tangalooma, a resort island that is known to travelers for its wild dolphin sanctuary.

The Spooky Island ferry on
Australia's gorgeous Gold Coast.

"It was a two-hour boat ride out from Brisbane," Matthew explains. "It's a solar-powered island, so the electricity would go out all the time. There are only like, eighteen people who live there, on the other side of the island from where we were shooting. We basically had to haul out everything that a movie set needs — habitation for one hundred and fifty people, food, generators to run the lights. We made this small village."

Set designers transformed the island into a dark and mysterious amusement park setting for the two weeks the cast and crew were there. It went from typical tropical resort to Mondavarious's Spooky Island. "Every morning I would ride to work, my buddy Scott would come pick me up in a Jeep, and we would ride along the beach and crashing waves for twenty minutes," Matthew recalls. "We were on the island for two weeks. Every night these wild dolphins would come into the bay and we'd get a chance to feed them."

"The island that stands in for Spooky Island was a paradise," Linda says. "I loved my life in Australia. It was beautiful. I was so close to the beach at all times and the beaches there are so vast and gorgeous. The sunsets are beautiful. One night, we had a huge lightning storm. You could see for miles whenever the lightning bolts came crashing down. They lit up the entire sky and came all the way down to the ground."

Tangalooma was the perfect setting for a movie, and it was also the perfect spot for the cast and crew to get to know one another. "On

A poster for Spooky Island.

Shaggy and Mary Jane, who jump on a motorbike to make their escape. The irony of the situation? Matthew had never ridden a motorbike before he arrived in Australia. But after a lot of practice, he felt confident enough he could handle the driving. But Isla wasn't so sure.

"I picked it up pretty quickly," Matthew explains. "Every time she got on the back of the bike she reminded me a hundred times 'please don't go too fast.' And then we start to get to

weekends we'd all get together and eat big meals and rent movies," Freddie says.

It's rare for a group to work so hard and yet have so much fun. But the Scooby crew was different, Raja says. "Because of the comedy, it's nice if there's a sense of humor on the set. Oftentimes, it was Matthew or Freddie keeping it light on the set, making everyone laugh and lifting the spirits," Raja says, smiling. "I would not want to make a movie where people aren't allowed to laugh on set. It's not worth it. You work too hard not to have fun when you can." As the months wore on, the group became even closer. "I think they did a lot of weekend outings. They are just a very tight-knit group, and it shows in the performance."

While they all got along well, Matthew confesses that there was a moment when he and Isla Fisher, who plays Shaggy's girlfriend Mary Jane, had a bit of a rough start. The scene involved a bunch of demons chasing

Matthew with his onscreen love interest, Isla Fisher (Mary Jane).

The bats were the least of the crew's worries. Because they were shooting in some remote locations, they were warned to beware of the country's many poisonous spiders, snakes, bees, and jelly fish, as well as to steer clear of other abundant Australian wildlife like kangaroos and wombats. "It's a very deadly continent, Australia," Matthew deadpans.

the speed where we're supposed to be and she's screaming in my ear. She's hurting me from behind, choking the wind out of me, screaming 'Oh my god! Please slow down!'" Matthew recalls, laughing. "I had to stop one day and tell her, 'Isla, the only thing that's scaring me is you screaming in my ears!'" Fortunately, they both made it through with flying colors — no bodily injuries or damaged eardrums.

But that doesn't mean the gang didn't encounter any other scary moments. "The first day I came onto location, we were at the Wow-O Toy Factory set, which was a power plant in the middle of a desolate area of Australia," Linda explains. "I looked above me and there's these giant fruit bats flying overhead. You know the screeching of the bats at the beginning of the Scooby-Doo episodes? I thought, 'How perfect!' I felt like I was in the cartoon."

Sarah and Linda joking around on set.

Producer Charles Roven, director Raja Gosnell, and actors Matthew Lillard, Freddie Prinze, Jr., Sarah Michelle Gellar, and Linda Cardellini at a press conference.

Luckily, the crew of native Australians steered the production away from any questionable situations. "The people are generous and kind and welcoming," says Sarah, who fell in love with the country years ago when she first traveled there.

And according to one fellow, the food is amazing. "I ate meals there I have never experienced anywhere else," Freddie says. "The people have a ton of pride in their coun-try and are willing to tell you all the tales over a good meal. The chefs were wonderfully creative and do things with fish you can't get in the States."

Indeed, the experience left everyone with an appetite for more. "We are set for a sequel if they want us to," Linda says. "We stayed in a place called Surfer's Paradise. If I have to work for half a year away from my loved ones, it might as well be in a place referred to as paradise."

The cast in one of their deadlier moments — captured by demons!

The beautiful Spooky Island resort.

CHAPTER EIGHT

WHAT'S YOUR SCOOBY I.Q.?

So you've seen the movie, you've read the book, and now you think you know everything there is to know about Scooby-Doo, right? Well, so did the actors who played Fred, Daphne, Velma, and Shaggy — until they took the Scooby-Doo I.Q. test! Take a look and see how many trivia questions you can answer correctly. Then turn to the next few pages to see how you scored. Compare your answers to Sarah's, Freddie's, Matthew's, and Linda's, and find out who your Scooby soulmate is. But no peeking!

1. What did the gang name their investigating agency?

2. When the group disbanded, where did Velma go to work?

3. What are the colors of the Mystery Machine?

4. Who created Scooby-Doo?

5. Which character always says "Jinkies"?

6. Where are Scooby Snacks made?

7. What is Shaggy's real full name?

8. What well-known singer had the words "scooby-dooby-doo" in a song?

   (Bonus question: What is the name of the song?)

9. Which famous radio DJ was the voice of the cartoon Shaggy for 22 years?

10. What type of tie does Fred Jones wear?

11. Which of the characters is a vegetarian?

12. One of the Scooby-Doo cartoon voice actors was nominated for an Emmy for a role in the television series *Life Goes On*. Who is it?

COMPARE YOUR ANSWERS WITH THE SCOOBY GANG'S!

SARAH (DAPHNE):

1. Mystery, Inc.

2. NASA

3. Blue, green, orange, and purple

4. William Hanna & Joseph Barbera

5. Velma

6. Hmmm . . . wasn't addressed in the cartoon that I know of.

7. Norville Rogers

8. Frank Sinatra. I don't know the song.

9. Casey Kasem

10. An ascot

11. Shaggy

12. Kellie Martin, but she was not in the original Scooby cartoon.

FREDDIE (FRED):

1. Mystery, Inc.

2. In the film, they say she goes off to do some work at NASA.

3. The Mystery Machine is blue and green and has orange letters. That is one groovy car. They actually had us driving around in a real one in the film. Matt loved that car. I bet he wishes he could have stolen that.

4. Don Messick came up with the idea originally.

5. Velma.

6. I guess they are made at the Scooby Snack Company's factory.

7. Norville Rogers

8. Frank Sinatra got pretty famous for throwing in that phrase and others like it into songs. I think he sang it in a song called "Lean Baby."

9. Casey Kasem.

10. An ascot. I had the inside track on that one.

11. I'd say Velma was the vegetarian. But that's a guess.

12. I really don't know.

MATTHEW (SHAGGY):

1. Mystery, Inc.

2. NASA

3. There are a lot of colors... green and gold and some orange, too. I lived in it.

4. Hanna-Barbera

5. Velma

6. I don't know

7. Norville Rogers

8. I don't know . . . oh, right. "Strangers in the Night."

9. Casey Kasem

10. An ascot

11. Shaggy

12. I have no idea. That's a stumper. That's new school Scooby-Doo, we're old school.

LINDA (YELMA):

1. Mystery, Inc.

2. NASA

3. Blue. The letters are orange and lime green.

4. Hanna-Barbera

5. My character, Velma. I also saved that as a souvenir. I say it a lot these days.

6. Daphne makes them.

7. Norville Shaggy Rogers

8. Frank Sinatra. He says that phrase in the middle of "Strangers in the Night."

9. Casey Kasem

10. Fred wears an ascot. It's red.

11. Shaggy

12. Kellie Martin

CORRECT ANSWERS:

Want to keep up on the latest Scooby-Doo news and information? Just log onto www.scoobydoo.warnerbros.com.

1. What did the gang name their investigating agency?

   Answer: Mystery, Inc.

   2. When the group disbanded, where did Velma go to work?

Answer: NASA

3. What are the colors of the Mystery Machine?

   Answer: The letters are orange, the rest of the van is turquoise and green.

4. Who created Scooby-Doo?

   Answer: The legendary animation team Joseph Hanna and William Barbera, also known as Hanna-Barbera. They also created the Flintstones and the Jetsons.

   5. Which character always says "Jinkies"?

Answer: Velma.

6. Where are Scooby Snacks made?

Answer: The Scooby Snacks factory.

7. What is Shaggy's real full name?

Answer: Norville Rogers.

8. What well-known singer had the words "scooby-dooby-doo" in a song?

(Bonus question: What is the name of the song?)

Answer: Frank Sinatra sang the words "scooby-dooby-doo" in the song "Strangers in the Night."

9. Which famous radio DJ was the voice of the cartoon Shaggy for 22 years?

Answer: Casey Kasem.

10. What type of tie does Fred Jones wear?

Answer: An ascot.

11. Which of the characters is a vegetarian?

Answer: Shaggy. (All those burgers you see him eating are veggie burgers.)

12. One of the Scooby-Doo cartoon voice actors was nominated for an Emmy for a role in the television series Life Goes On. Who is it?

Answer: Kellie Martin, who also appeared on ER. She voiced Daphne in A Pup Named Scooby-Doo from 1985-1986.